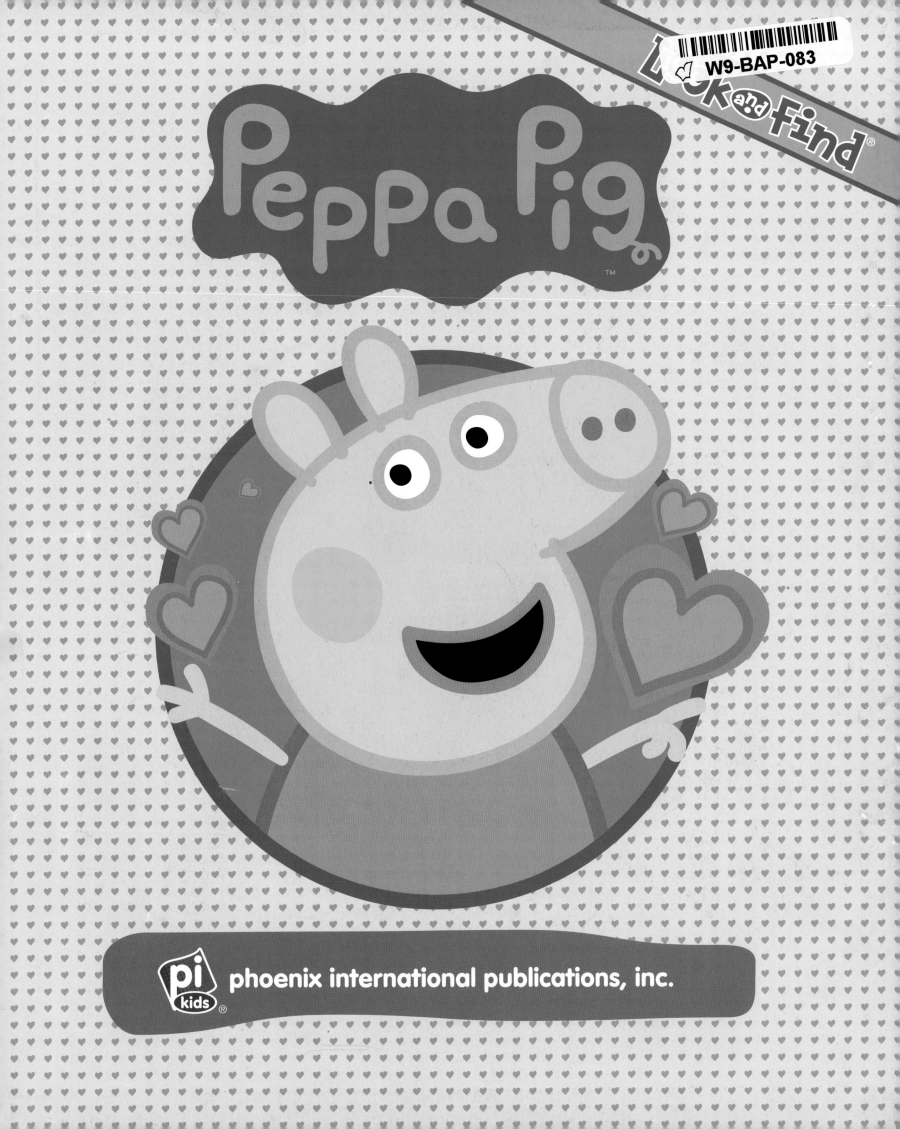

Look and Find®

# Peppa Pig™

phoenix international publications, inc.
pi kids®

Good morning! This is Peppa Pig's room. And George's too. It's a little bit messy. Will you help Peppa find these toys and tidy up?

teddy bear

dinosaur

bus

horn

car

jack-in-the-box

It's breakfast time for the chickens! Peppa and George go to Granny Pig's house to help her with the feeding. Will you look for these things while the chickens eat?

watering can

basket

spade

pails

broom

seeds

Peppa loves going to playgroup! Today is arts and crafts day. While Peppa paints, find and point to these classroom objects:

map

this flower painting

clock

globe

this book

Newton's cradle

Hop, hop, hop! Peppa plays hopscotch with her friends, and then twirls a hoop while she waits for her turn. See if you can spot these other things to play with:

golf ball

soccer ball

bicycle

whistle

jump rope

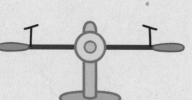

seesaw

Playing makes Peppa extra hungry! Come into the kitchen and get ready for dinner by finding these yummy things to eat and drink:

salad

apple

slice of pizza

banana

cup of tea

corn on the cob

Peppa and her friends are practicing a play! While they try on different costumes, look for these fun props and decorations:

ukulele

juggling balls

drum

top hat

confetti

yellow balloon

Daddy Pig is a bit of an expert at storytelling. Look around as he reads to Peppa and George and try to find these family photos:

Daddy Pig

Peppa

Baby Peppa

George

Mummy Pig

Granny and Grandpa Pig

Peppa Pig loves muddy puddles! Remember, if you are jumping up and down in muddy puddles, you must wear your boots. Hats are useful, too, when it's chilly. Will you help Peppa and her friends find these?

Go back to Peppa's bedroom and find these things that rhyme:

head and bed     block and clock
ball and wall     cat and hat
train and plane

Visit Granny Pig again and see if there are more...

...clouds or flowers?
...chickens or flowers?
...flowers or pigs?
...chickens or clouds?
...pigs or chickens?

Skip back to playgroup and count these craft supplies:

1 tube of paint
2 paintbrushes
3 tubs of clay
4 colored pencils
5 crayons

Take another turn at the playground and look for things in each of these colors:

yellow     green
blue     white
pink     purple

Return to the kitchen and
find things that are:

on the stove
next to the bulletin board
above the window
under Mummy Pig
behind the pasta jar

Peppa starts with P!
Prance back to the play
practice and find other
things that start with p:

pirate
police officer
postal carrier
prince
Polynesian Princess Peppa

Snuggle up on the living
room sofa and spot things
in these shapes:

circle
square
star
heart
oval
diamond

Splash back to the muddy
puddle and find these
matching pairs:

pair of flowers
pair of butterflies
pair of bees
pair of boots
pair of Zebra twins